# Missing Time

# Femdom Hypnosis and Mind Control Micro-Fiction

## S.B.

## Disclaimer

This is a work of fiction. Names, characters, business, events, and incidents are the products of the author's imagination. Any resemblance to actual persons, living or dead, or actual events is purely coincidental. All characters are over 18.

*Time flies when you're in a trance.*

*Thank you to all patrons of Spell... B-O-U-N-D.*

# Table of Contents


- Introduction – 1

- Perfect - 2
- Empty Chest - 3
- Say Something - 4
- Hypnotic Collection - 5
- Passive and Obedient - 6
- Whatever You Want - 7
- A Pair - 8
- Harry's Routine - 9
- Failed Run - 10
- Salty - 11
- Sick Mind - 12
- Her Secret - 13
- Like the First Time - 14
- So Weird - 15
- Anything for Pleasure - 16
- Mistress of Beasts - 17
- Hypnotic Accident - 18
- Played - 19
- Give Them Hell - 20
- What Did You Do? - 21
- Ketchup and Hypnosis - 22
- Work Harder - 23
- Bitch Mode - 24
- Too Many Hands - 25
- Mistress Loves Spirals - 26
- I'd Forgotten - 27
- Just Nice? - 28
- Recurring Pattern - 29
- Cleansing - 30

- Something's Wrong - 31
- Live a Little - 32
- Her Divine Right - 33
- Good Drone - 34
- Real Food - 35
- Femdom Hypnosis Is Everywhere - 36
- Mental Lobotomy - 37
- New Toy - 38
- The Ring - 39
- Tired - 40
- Amazing Feet - 41
- Let it All Fade - 42
- Alone in the Light - 43
- Paper on Evolution - 44
- It Will Never Happen - 45
- Ready for Service - 46
- What Else Have You Forgotten? - 47
- Nerfed - 48
- Some Things Never Change… - 49
- Missing Time - 50
- Walking Away - 51
- Nasty Thing - 52
- Pissed - 53
- Not Herself - 54
- You Fell for it Again! - 55
- Star Athlete - 56

- Conclusion - 57

# Introduction

People say time is a constant, and yet it moves too quickly or too slowly when you're in a trance. In the realms of hypnotic fantasies, everything bends and shifts and the impossible becomes a reality. It's time to explore them once more in another selection of tantalizing micro-fiction.

The stories in this volume were written between February 7th, and April 2nd, 2022, and published on my personal website – Spell... B-O-U-N-D – as part of my daily 55 Words Challenge that's been running for more than six years now.  Join the fun with our suggestions and let's continue to be creative together.

## Perfect

Carl couldn't stop staring at Joan's eyes. They were perfect.

"You love them," she said.

"I love them," he repeated.

"They control your mind."

"They control my mind."

"They want you to take off your clothes."

Carl nodded silently and undid his pants while the rest of her family cheered. She was definitely a natural.

## Empty Chest

Hank was furious. X had marked the spot, but for what?

"Fuck! What am I going to do with an empty treasure chest?" he grumbled.

"Who says it was empty?" a sultry voice echoed on the sands beneath his feet.

He only saw a glimpse of the pirate captain's ghost before she pillaged his mind.

## Say Something!

"You're infuriating!" Mark grumbled.

"What's wrong with him?" Nia asked.

"He's upset I won't undo his chastity triggers," Laura replied.,

"Okay, but why is he shouting at a mannequin?"

"I hypnotized him into thinking that's me, so I don't have to deal with his shit."

"Say something, damn it!" he shouted.

The two women laughed.

**Hypnotic Collection**

Jonah gasped upon seeing Anne's hypnotic collection. There were pocket watches, rings, pendants, and countless other mind-melting paraphernalia, all whispering his name.

"Wow! Have you used them all before?"

"Not on the same subject..." she smiled. "Will you be the first?"

He nodded, immediately canceling all plans. It was going to be a wonderful weekend.

**Passive and Obedient**

Enidin's jaw slacked when he reached the hive's main hall and saw The Queen Bee, her enchanting smile defying all resistance. Immediately, his cock got hard beyond his control.

"What's happening?" he mumbled.

"Pheromones," she replied. "They keep drones passive and obedient. Kneel."

The mercenary complied as she laughed. Humans were so easy to tame!

## Whatever You Want

"I'll pay you whatever you want," Ted said.

"No!" Victoria replied. "You can't bribe me into hypnotizing you."

"I'll max out every credit card for you! Just one more time, please."

"You're addicted. Not today and not ever. We'll talk when you're clean."

She turned his back on him while he broke down in tears.

## A Pair

Gavin sat by the door, empty, defeated, wanting nothing or no one.

"You really fried his mind this time," Nadine said.

"Yep," Wanda agreed.

"Did he want this?"

"Not really, but you have to admit he makes a good ornament."

"A pair would be better."

"You're right," Wanda drew a pocket watch from her cleavage.

## Harry's Routine

Harry's routine was unbreakable. Every day at 7 pm he sat on a park bench, waiting for the impossible.

"Why does he do that?" Gloria asked.

"Mistress Aurora programmed him that way," Luke replied.

"But isn't she...?"

"Dead? Yes. It's been two years, but his mind still hasn't processed it, so..."

The two friends sighed.

## Failed Run

Mark laid the controller on the floor. "Not again!" he said.

"Another failed run?" Pamela asked.

"Yeah. I'm always hypnotized by a vampire on the 13th floor. Rogue-like, my ass!"

"Don't complain. You love hypnosis."

"True, but..."

"Next time will be different."

She was right. He was hypnotized by a vampire on the 1st floor.

## Salty

Walter stared in awe at the video on Gemma's phone. There he was, kneeling before her next to his brother.

"When did this happen?" he asked.

"Yesterday."

"But we weren't together yesterday."

"The camera doesn't lie. You're both wonderful subjects... and here comes the best part."

"Fuck!" he exclaimed. No wonder his mouth tasted salty.

## Sick Mind

Jonah and Richard stared at the computer screen.

"This is terrifying," the first said.

"Agreed. What sick mind comes up with this?"

"I thought you liked porn, boys," Flora chuckled.

"Only femdom porn. Men dominating women? Gross!" Richard replied.

"Spoken like true brainwashed bitches..." she thought. They were almost ready to meet her strapon collection.

## Her Secret

Paul squinted when he saw the footage for the nth time. It was true. The store manager was an extraterrestrial.

"Liked what you saw?" Dana asked, her eyes glowing green.

"What are you?"

"Don't worry about that."

"If you hurt me, everyone will know."

"Not if you forget everything."

The security room faded to white.

## Like the First Time

Martha caressed Jamie's hair and asked,

"Was it as good for you as it was for me, baby?"

"I can't remember," Jamie replied.

"Really? You're so lucky!"

"Why?"

"The next time I hypnotize you it will be like the first again..."

"You're probably right."

"As always."

Martha's hands fluttered soundlessly as Jamie sank once more.

## So Weird

Jane stared at the robot.

"This is so weird! Why does it look like your ex-husband?" she asked.

"You know why," Lucy grinned.

"Fuck! Is this what you do to those you hate now?"

"Sometimes, but it's fun to do it to friends too."

"What do you... oh!

Jane screamed as her hands became silver.

## Anything for Pleasure

It was not the news Martha wanted.

"Permanent?" she gasped.

"Yes," Dr. Summer replied.

"But wasn't this treatment going well?"

"Your boyfriend is too resistant. There's no other way."

"How much then?"

"Two pills in the morning, afternoon, and night. and you have a slave for life."

"Okay," she sighed. "Anything for pleasure."

He soundlessly agreed.

## Mistress of Beasts

It was too late for Timothy. Falling to the ground, he begged,

"Run!"

"But Tim..." Harriet said.

"Run and don't look back! She's already in my mind. RUN!"

Harriet dashed across the forest, the blood-red full moon hanging above her head. Inhuman growls cut the air all around. The Mistress of Beasts was hunting again.

## Hypnotic Accident

Walter found Aaron waiting for him outside the hospital, a bloody bandage on his forehead.

"Are you okay, mate?" he asked.

"Yeah. It looks worse than what really is."

"What happened?"

"Hypnosis accident."

"Huh?"

"I was entranced when Jade tried her new fucking machine on me."

"And...?"

"I forgot where my ass was."

Walter chuckled.

## Played

"It's finally here!" Sam exclaimed as he unwrapped his early birthday gift. The new Black Queen game was all he wanted... if he could make it past the cover.

Gorgeous violet eyes emerged from the black background immediately dictating his fate. He would not play but be played instead.

Cock in hand, he began stroking.

## Give Them Hell

The purple mind-controlling gas crept through the vents of Bill's apartment.

"Fuck, it's already here!" he said.

"What do we do?" His younger, brother, Charles, asked.

"Anything but standing still. Let's give those bitches hell before they enslave us. Are you in?"

"Hell yeah?"

Shotgun in hand, Bill rushed to face the gynoid alien invaders.

## What Did You Do?

Mark emptied his glass while Natalie chuckled.

"What are you laughing at?" he asked.

"Nothing," she shrugged.

"Liar. I know how your mind works. What did you do?"

"Guess."

Mark scratched his chin. She loved hypnosis, and confusion was her favorite weapon which could only mean...

"This wasn't milk."

"Nope."

Mark rushed to the bathroom.

## Ketchup and Hypnosis

Mark saw his older sister holding a knife and her boyfriend covering his bloody crotch and gasped.

"You didn't..."

"Relax, it's just ketchup and hypnosis," Andie smirked.

"Thank God! I thought..."

"So does he. He'll be a good slave from now on."

Mark gulped, making a mental note to never piss her off for real.

# Work Harder

The last day of the month meant fresh money in the bank. Paul logged in to his account to check the balance and his earnings were gone in a blink.

"I... what?"

"Well done, slave," his ruthless hypnotic findom texted him. "Work harder for me."

"Yes, Mistress," he drooled. Double shifts sounded a good idea.

## Bitch Mode

"What the fuck?" Mark gasped when he saw Ethan's new toy.

"It's a fembot," his friend said.

"But why?"

"It was cheap, and I thought it would be fun."

"And is it?"

"Yes, especially when Bitch Mode is activated."

"Which is...?

Spiraling red eyes burrowed into their minds, forcing them to kneel. The party began.

## Too Many Hands

Gary used one hand to masturbate and the other to scratch his nose. One more rubbed his balls while the fourth fondled his ass.

"Wait," he thought as another slid down his back while the last caressed his hair.

Brother and sisters smiled vacantly, happy in trance. The three thralls continued to play for Mistress.

## Mistress Loves Spirals

Clark laid down the brush and asked,

"What do you think?"

"It's... hmmm... a different paint job, for sure," John replied, staring at the front of the house.

"Mistress loves spirals."

"Mistress? Don't you mean Ally?"

"That's what I said... Mistress."

"Can't say her real name anymore, huh?"

"Mistress," Clark repeated, going deeper and deeper.

## I'd Forgotten

Mario rolled in bed, nostrils taken over by a delicious scent.

"I'd forgotten how nice your hair smells," he said.

"Did you forget anything else?" Tara asked.

"Should I?" he mumbled.

"Not tonight, my pet," she cooed.

The next day, he forgot his name, but she took care of it. Marina rose from the bed.

## Just Nice?

Everything about Martha was nice but nothing more. She had nice tits, nice legs, a nice ass...

"Just nice?" she grumbled.

"Yeah," Darren shrugged and looked away.

A scorned woman is a terrible thing, especially if she's a witch. He should have known better.

The next day, he woke up screaming, buried in his boobs.

## Recurring Pattern

Paul stared at his blog's stats, noticing the recurring pattern. Up one day, down in the next. Up... down... Up... down... like when Margaret fractionated him into a drooling mess. It was all so... so...

"Look who's already got himself ready for me..." she whispered in his ear.

He smiled vacantly, ready to be taken.

## Cleansing

It was raining again.

Heavy drops landed on Mark's face, arms, and legs, washing the dirt from his face and all impure thoughts from his mind.

"Do you understand now?" the voice of the Goddess. "Surrender."

Mark dropped to his knees and smiled. The radioactive man was gone, only the loyal and obedient slave remained.

# Something's Wrong

Johanna looked in the mirror and shook her head. Something was wrong!

"What's the matter?" Alicia asked.

"I feel like something doesn't add up, but not sure what it is."

"You're just tired, dear. It's been a long week."

"Are you sure?"

"Positive."

"Okay."

John returned to bed and closed his eyes. The feminization continued.

## Live a Little

The suspended bridge stretched over a giant abyss.

"Come on!" Laura shouted from the other side. "What are you afraid of?"

"What if I fall?" Jack asked, knees trembling.

"I'll catch you."

"Do you promise?"

"Yes. Adventure is fun, sweetie. Live a little."

Jack nodded and took the first step forward into a blissful trance.

## Her Divine Right

"BILL!" Jack shouted.

"What's wrong?" his friend murmured.

"Your wife is fucking the neighbor on the porch, and you're just going to sit there and do nothing?"

"Goddess fucks whoever she wants. It's her divine right."

"What? Brainwashed much?"

Bill nodded, the enslaving mantras still fresh in his mind. Smiling, he continued enjoying the show.

## Good Drone

Terrence was a good, brainwashed drone. He did everything his sister, Margaret, wanted.

She told him to jerk off and he jerked off.

She told him to pay for her dates and he paid for her dates.

One day, she told him to jump off his company's building.

Inheriting his entire fortune never felt better.

**Real Food**

Paul threw the ice cream away. His once favorite treat no longer tasted the same.

"Are you feeling okay, bud?" his friend, Jack, asked.

"No. I need real food right now!" Paul screamed.

"Calm down. What are you talking about?"

"Mistress' pussy," Paul left the restaurant and ran to his apartment to book another session.

## Femdom Hypnosis is Everywhere

The series finale had been a disappointment. Main characters dying, a major cliffhanger... but what really irked Oliver was not knowing

".... if Margaret hypnotized Troy or not."

"She did," Samantha replied.

"How can you be sure?"

"Femdom hypnosis is everywhere."

He nodded as he stared into her eyes. The real show was about to begin.

## Mental Lobotomy

The ray gun completed its firing sequence. Matthew stared blankly, a black circle on his wrinkled forehead.

"All done," Angie said.

"Wait, it worked?" her sister Ava, asked.

"Of course. Mental lobotomy, instant slave."

"Great, but let's not get carried away with this power, okay?"

"Sure," Angie smirked, already imagining the city at her feet.

## New Toy

The dog wagged his tail by the front door. His owner was home and had brought him a present. She was so sweet! He did a happy dance around her feet and then ran outside to show off the new toy.

All the neighbors saw was a hypnotized man with a bone in his mouth.

## The Ring

The silver ring shone with unnatural light, calling Sandra by name.

"Is this really happening?" she asked, approaching the piece of jewelry forgotten in the park near her house.

"Take me and find out," it said.

Sandra touched it, sparks of ancient power flowing through her trembling body. The Goddess had chosen her new slave.

## Tired

He was tired. Of the world, the people in it, the miseries all around.

She was tired too, but this was a date for celebration and green still means hope.

When their hands met, they danced together in a verdant field, and in her eyes, he finally found solace and warmth.

Happy St. Patrick's Day!

# Amazing Feet

Eliza's feet were amazing, its delicate arches making Trevor's mouth salivate. The weird thing was that he wasn't into feet.

"You are now," she declared, waving her purple painted toes before his drooping eyes and if she said so, it was surely true.

Trevor dropped to his knees and worshipped his Goddess all weekend long.

## Let it All Fade

Amy gently directed Peter's hand.

"That's it, almost there... now press that button and clear all those nasty things from your mi, I mean, computer. Let it all fade, everything going blank...

"Hmmm, we're still talking about cookies, right?" he asked.

"What else?" Amy smiled, continuing the induction. His thoughts were as good as hers.

## Alone in the Light

Nothingness. Pure virginal white of no substance or consequence. The more John walked forward the less he moved at all.

"So, this is the afterlife," he thought. "Boring as shit."

"Not for long," whispered a choir of feminine voices eager to take his body for a spin. He wasn't alone in the light after all.

## Paper on Evolution

"First, Man created weapons out of bone. Then, Fire was discovered. As centuries went by, the first mining operations began. Women discovered the power of hypnotic crystals, and men happily submitted to the collar," Erin concluded.

"That's your paper on evolution?" Professor Morris asked. "It's preposterous."

"Says the slave kneeling at my feet..." she laughed.

## It Will Never Happen

"I already said you can't hypnotize me. It will never happen, got it?" Magnus said.

"Absolutely," Jessica yawned. "It's cool that you'll never resist."

"That's not what I said!"

"It's what I heard. Is the rant over?"

"Yes."

"Good."

She snapped her fingers and dropped instantly. He would never be hypnotized... until the next time.

**Ready for Service**

Garrett stumbled by the porch, hands shaking. He could feel his consciousness slipping away.

"Not again!" he screamed.

His muscles stiffened, eyes going blank. He turned around and approached the limo parked at the end of the street.

"Slut ready for service," he declared, picking up his new latex dress. Mistress's new clients were waiting.

## What Else Have You Forgotten?

The death screen flashed again on Jarod's TV.

"Fuck this! I'm out!" he exclaimed.

"Quitting so soon?" his girlfriend, Melanie, asked.

"Yeah, I think I've forgotten how to play these games."

"What else have you forgotten?"

"I... hmmm... who are you again?"

"You don't need to remember that..." she grinned.

He still doesn't. Game Over!

**Nerfed**

Elmer stood passively against the kitchen wall, unflinching.

"What happened to your husband?" Catherine asked, drinking lemon tea.

"He's been nerfed," Lucy replied.

"Nerfed?"

"Yes. His complaints were rendered ineffective, and his resistance is gone too."

"How?"

"I drugged his tea when he wasn't looking."

Catherine stared at the pot on the table and gulped.

## Some Things Never Change...

"Have you heard from Kevin?" Caitlin asked.

"He's still at the hospital," Deanna replied.

"Do you think the doctors suspect anything?"

"If they did, the cops would already be here."

"Still, you need to be more careful next time."

"I will, but in the meantime..."

"Yes?"

"I'm brainwashing your brother tomorrow."

"Some things never change..."

## Missing Time

David was shocked. The clock atop his nightstand couldn't be lying, right?

"How did I lose so much time?" he asked.

"We've entered Daylight Savings," Karen replied.

"That explains one hour, but what about the other ten?"

"You're a wonderful subject," she held a crystal pendulum before his eyes.

So true. Another day was gone.

# Walking Away

"No, Anne."

"But Walter..."

"I already said no. I'm done doing things your way, so this is over."

"You don't get to walk away from me."

"I just did. Goodbye."

Walter left the house and entered Justine's car, smiling.

"Thank you for building my confidence to do this."

"You're welcome," she said.

Femdom hypnosis forever.

## Nasty Thing

"Welcome back," Dr. Winters said.

"Was the operation...?" Greg asked.

"... a success? Definitely!" she showed him a jar with a strange creature inside.

"What is that?!"

"Ego Parasite. This nasty thing was making you resistant to my control but now..." she snapped her fingers. "Kneel, slave."

"Yes, Mistress."

"Perfect," she said, reaching for a collar.

## Pissed

"You look pissed, Joe."

"You have no idea, Mark."

"What happened?"

"Kimberly got inside my head again and had me masturbate all night long."

"Seriously? That doesn't sound too bad."

"Then get ready to think differently."

"Why do you say that?"

"That's not cream in your coffee."

Mark rushed to the bathroom to clean himself.

## Not Herself

Nathan glanced at Judy.

"I'm telling you, she's not herself," he said.

"For the last time, your sister isn't possessed by a ghost!" Tim noted.

"But..."

"But nothing. Let's clear your head, okay?"

A couple of drinks later, Nathan no longer believed his delusions. It was obvious ghosts weren't real.

Witches on the other hand...

## You Fell for it Again!

Dennis exited the store carrying more bags than he could handle.

"Correct me if I'm wrong, but didn't you say your financial dominatrix days were over?" he asked.

Lucy lowered her sunglasses and smirked.

"Yes, but it's April Fools'. Don't worry, we're done."

"Thank God!"

"Ah, you fell for it again!"

The shopping spree continued.

## Star Athlete

Timothy was a star athlete. He knew Kung Fu, held swimming records, and could run after a speeding bike without breaking a sweat. His results seemed too good to be true and only got better each day.

Some suspected drugs were involved but the truth was simpler His girlfriend knew hypnosis.

Time for another session.

# Conclusion

Now that you've finished reading these tales, time will flow normally again… perhaps. The truth is, once you've tasted an altered state of mind, you always want to come back for more. Luckily, you can.

Be sure to visit my personal website - https://www.sbspellbound.net - every single day. Many more secrets are waiting for you there and you may even have your personal fantasies come true. Support my creative efforts if you wish to see more. Have fun.

www.ingramcontent.com/pod-product-compliance
Lightning Source LLC
Chambersburg PA
CBHW071448150726
48000CB00006B/2481